WOULD YOU LIKE TO PLAY **HIDE & SEEK** IN THIS BOOK WITH LOVABLE, FURRY OLD **GROVER?**

featuring Jim Henson's Muppet

DID YOU COUNT TO TEN?

written by Jon Stone • illustrated by Mike Smollin

RANDOM HOUSE/CHILDREN'S TELEVISION WORKSHOP

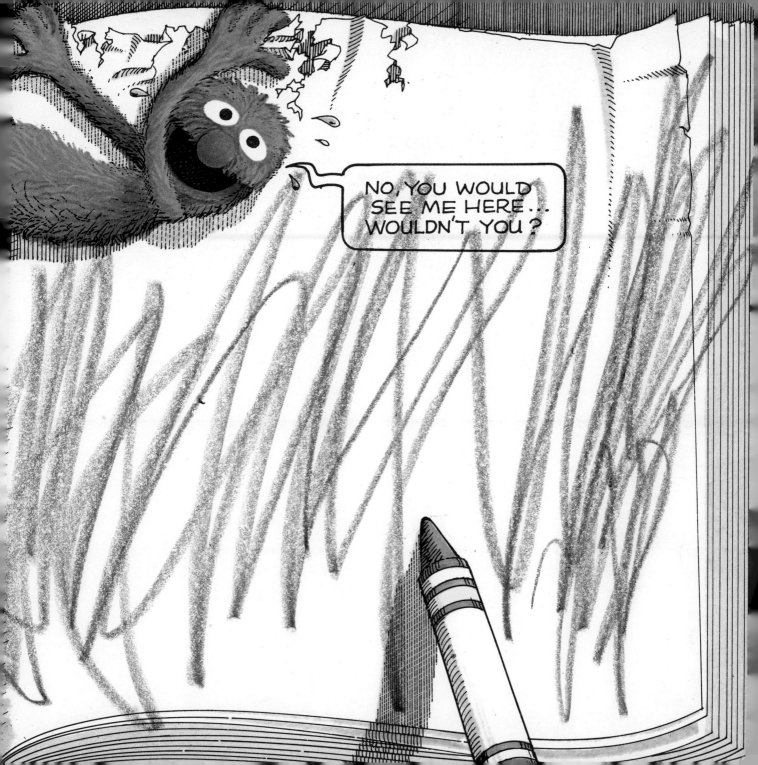

DOWN HERE AT THE **BOTTOM** OF THE PAGE ?

NO!!

DO YOU KNOW SOMETHING ?
THERE ARE NOT MANY PLACES
FOR A MONSTER TO HIDE
IN A BOOK LIKE THIS.

I, LOVABLE, SMART OLD GROVER WILL SAY MANY, MANY, MANY WORDS AND THEN THERE WILL BE LOTS OF THESE FUNNY WHITE BALLOONS WITH WORDS IN THEM, AND I CAN HIDE BEHIND THEM!